# Freckles and Jane

Margery Cuyler

# Freckles and Jane

## Illustrated by Leslie Holt Morrill

FRECKLES

Henry Holt and Company     New York

Published by Henry Holt and Company, Inc.,
115 West 18th Street, New York, New York 10011.
Published in Canada by Fitzhenry & Whiteside Limited,
195 Allstate Parkway, Markham, Ontario L3R 4T8.

Library of Congress Cataloging-in-Publication Data
Cuyler, Margery.
Freckles and Jane.
Summary: Jane dislikes her friend Willie's dog
Freckles until Freckles defends her from a big mean dog.
[1. Dogs—Fiction] I. Morrill, Leslie H., ill.
II. Title.
PZ7.C997Fs   1990        [E]        88-32068
ISBN 0-8050-0643-5

Henry Holt books are available at special discounts
for bulk purchases for sales promotions, premiums,
fund-raising, or educational use. Special editions
or book excerpts can also be created to specification.

For details contact:

Special Sales Director
Henry Holt and Company, Inc.
115 West 18th Street
New York, New York 10011

First Edition
Printed in the United States of America
1 3 5 7 9 10 8 6 4 2

*to Willie Charczuk,*
*for whom this story was written*
*—M.C.*

Freckles was Willie's best friend.
  He was always there when Willie needed him.

If Willie got cold, Freckles curled up under his feet like a warm, comfy pillow.

If Willie felt sad, Freckles brought him a ball, and they played until Willie felt better.

If Willie overslept, Freckles licked his face until he woke up.

Jane was Willie's friend too. She lived next door. She didn't like Freckles.

"His tail looks like an old string," she said. "His bones smell, and he makes me sneeze."

"It's too bad you feel that way," said Willie. "You and Freckles could have a lot of fun."

On Saturday, Freckles was going to be three years old. Willie decided to give him a birthday party. He invited his mother and father. And . . . he invited Jane. "Maybe she'll learn to like Freckles," thought Willie. "She just needs to spend more time with him."

All week Willie worked on the party. He decorated the playroom. He made Freckles a birthday card in the shape of a bone. At the last minute, he filled Freckles' bowl with cookies and cake. Then it was time for the party.

Mom and Dad arrived with presents. Mom made Freckles a new bed. Dad bought him a leather collar with his name on it. Willie gave Freckles a big rawhide bone. "It's good for your teeth," he said.

Jane bought Freckles a can of flea powder.
"Because you're always scratching," Jane told Freckles.
Freckles lay down with his head on his paws. His body sagged and his ears drooped.

"You hurt his feelings," said Willie.
"I can't help it," said Jane. "He's disgusting." Then she sneezed.

A few days later Jane came over to Willie's house again.
"Do you want to go on a picnic?" she asked.
"Not unless we bring Freckles," said Willie.
Jane hesitated. "Can you leave his bone behind?"
"No," said Willie. "His bone comes too."
"Will you give him a flea bath first?" pleaded Jane.
"No," said Willie. "He comes the way he is, fleas and all."

Jane sighed loudly. "Okay," she said at last.
Freckles jumped up and licked her face.
"Yuck," said Jane. "Your tongue's like a wet sponge."

Jane and Willie got on their bikes and started pedaling.
Freckles ran behind them.

As they turned the corner, a big dog sprang out of the bushes.
"Grrrr!" it growled, snapping at Jane's ankles.
"Get away!" yelled Jane.

Freckles barked. His fur stood up. The big dog bared his teeth. They were as sharp as thorns. He jumped at Freckles.

They rolled into a ball of snarling, yapping fur.
"Help!" screamed Willie.

A woman ran out of her garage, carrying a hose.

*Swoosh!* She sprayed the dogs, and they sprang apart. Freckles whimpered. His ear was bleeding.

"Poor Freckles!" said Jane.

"He's shaking!" said Willie. He put Freckles' leash on.

"Let's get out of here," he cried.

"I'm so sorry," said the woman, yanking her dog toward the house. "My dog got loose. Is yours all right?"

But Freckles and Willie were running down the block. Jane followed them with the bikes.

When they got home, Willie checked Freckles from head to toe. Only his ear was hurt. Willie dabbed it with peroxide so it wouldn't get infected.

"You were lucky, Freckles," said Jane. "And you were very brave."
She patted Freckles on the head. "You still need a bath," she said.
Willie groaned, but Freckles wagged his tail.
"See?" said Jane. "He knows it will make him feel better."

So Willie and Jane scrubbed Freckles until he smelled like fresh laundry. He ran around in circles, shaking his fur.

When he was dry, Jane said, "Look at his tail. It's almost fluffy."

"And he's stopped scratching," said Willie, dabbing more peroxide on his ear.

"Maybe I won't sneeze anymore," said Jane.

She brought Freckles a bowl of water and tied a ribbon around
his neck. "Happy late birthday," she said. Then she sneezed.

"I guess the bath didn't work. But it doesn't matter," she said, patting his head. "Freckles is cute."

Freckles licked her face. Then he curled up under her feet like a warm, comfy pillow.